Animal Attention

Written by John Block

and Illustrated by Oren Otter

Copyright 2019, ISBN 978-1-7336019-1-7

"Everybody's busy today, except me."

"Mom is in the garden dusting tomatoes, whatever that is?"

"Brother and sister are reading books,
but their books don't have pictures."

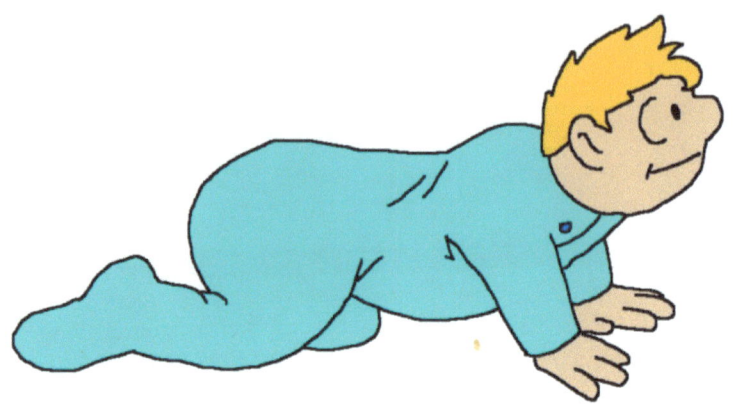

"I'll crawl over to Dad and help him write."

"He doesn't notice me!"

"What if I become a floppy-eared dog and touch his hand with my cold, wet nose?"

"Aw shucks! He'd move his hand."

"Maybe I'll turn into a slithering snake and wrap around the lamp by his desk."

"Get

off

the

lamp,

Son."

"I could become a royal romping reindeer and move his desk with my antlers."

"But I might grow an antler!"

"If I was a skunk, he would notice me. He he."

"But what if he has a stuffed-up nose and can't smell a thing?"

"If I was an anteater, I'd stick my tongue out this far .....

… and grab that pencil out of his hand."

"Maybe a crocodile clamp with some terrible teeth would get his attention."

"Ouch! That would be the hardest foot I've ever tasted."

"I could be a platypus and say, 'Excuse me, would you like to go swimming?'"

"It's wet, but am I swimming?"

"That's it. I'll be a porcupine and lay on the seat of his chair."

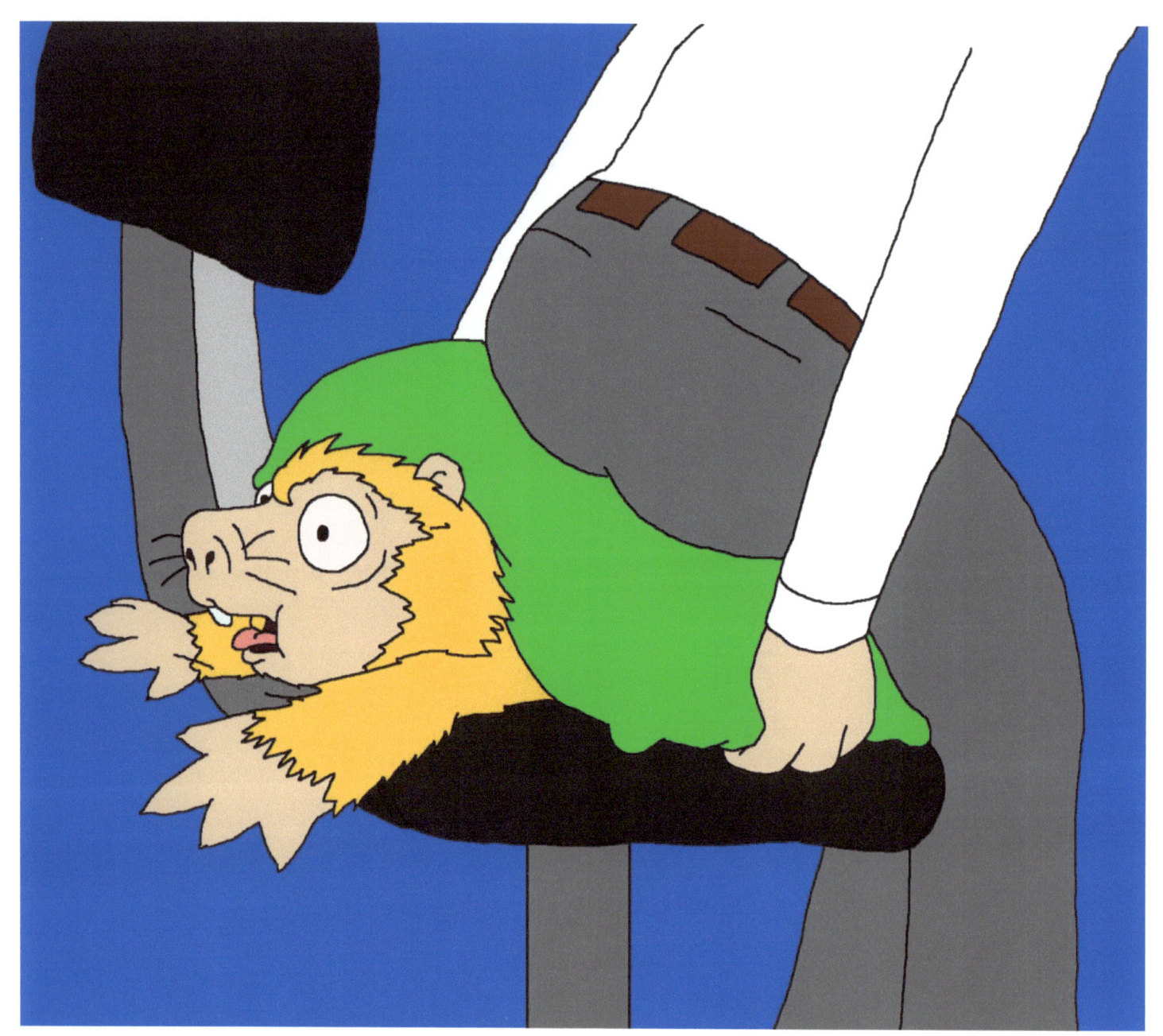

"He'd probably sit on a pillow, and I'd get squashed!"

"I guess the only thing left to do is howl like a yowling coyote."

"Son, is that you?"

"Let's go out and play, Dad."

And we played and played… and played.

"Thanks, Dad."   "Let's go in, Son."

"I think I'll curl up on Dad's shoulder and be like a … purr."

The End

Author John Block lives with his wife Mary Lou, two dogs (Banjo and Emmy), and a varying and sometimes large number of farm cats.

Illustrator Oren Otter lives with his wife Fnaire and their six children who are all very talented at being different animals.